PERFECTION

written by
T.G. BIRDSONG

illustrations by KARINE MAKARTICHAN
forward by REGGIE SANDERS

Perfection
©2024 Tracy BirdSong

ISBN: 979-8-35093-551-6

Dedicated to my little loves, Jeremiah Aaron (J'aaron), and Mary Isabelle.
Be Sweet, Be Kind, Be Brave

FORWARD BY REGGIE SANDERS

Perfection is perception, of course. The way that we see the world and the beautiful people in it comes from the places we've been, the pain we've endured, and the progress that we have made: and all of that is personal before it is public.

In this Sophomore book, Tracy BirdSong discusses the myths and stigmata that often surround autistic families through education and advocacy. She emotionally teaches the reader invaluable lessons through the grace and love of the little sister of the main character.

Following the path of education has always been the most effective way to mobilize people. More specifically, in this book, I am reminded of growing up as an advocate for my brother Demetrius who likewise has apraxia. It can be challenging for families with brothers and sisters with special needs to find creative ways to help them communicate and be heard at the same time.

While reading *Perfection*, I noted how many times my mother and I had to explain, assist, and protect my brother from those who didn't understand him-all while learning and growing ourselves.

The autism community has for years had to stand up for ourselves, and it's refreshing to read a book that is designed for those on the outside looking in at how we as families navigate those spaces. Through colored illustrations using appropriate definitions, Perfection is a great read.

Whether in public and school libraries, or from the comfort of your own homes, in reading this book, you will be enlightened to learn, educated to share, and empowered to act.

Reggie Sanders

They say my brother is autistic (au T is tic),

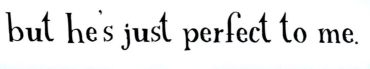

but he's just perfect to me.

I've heard them use the word apraxia (a PRAX i a), which just means he can't speak. Although he tries real hard.

He goes to **speech therapy** twice a week

He goes to OT, occupational therapy, too.
It's more than just teaching him to tie his shoe.

They teach him how to JUMP

and HOP

and SKIP

and how to walk with his toes not TIPPED!

I've heard them say he's **stimming** when he shakes a string up and down.

I think he's conducting an orchestra
and marching them through the town!

Sometimes he rubs his fists on his cheecks and jaw real fast. That's when I get ready for that high-pitched, squealing BLAST!

That is stimming, too.
It means he's happy through and through!

OCD, obsessive compulsive disorder,
can be part of Autism, too.
He keeps his room neat and tidy

not messy like I do!

and **OVER**,

like an echo through the house.

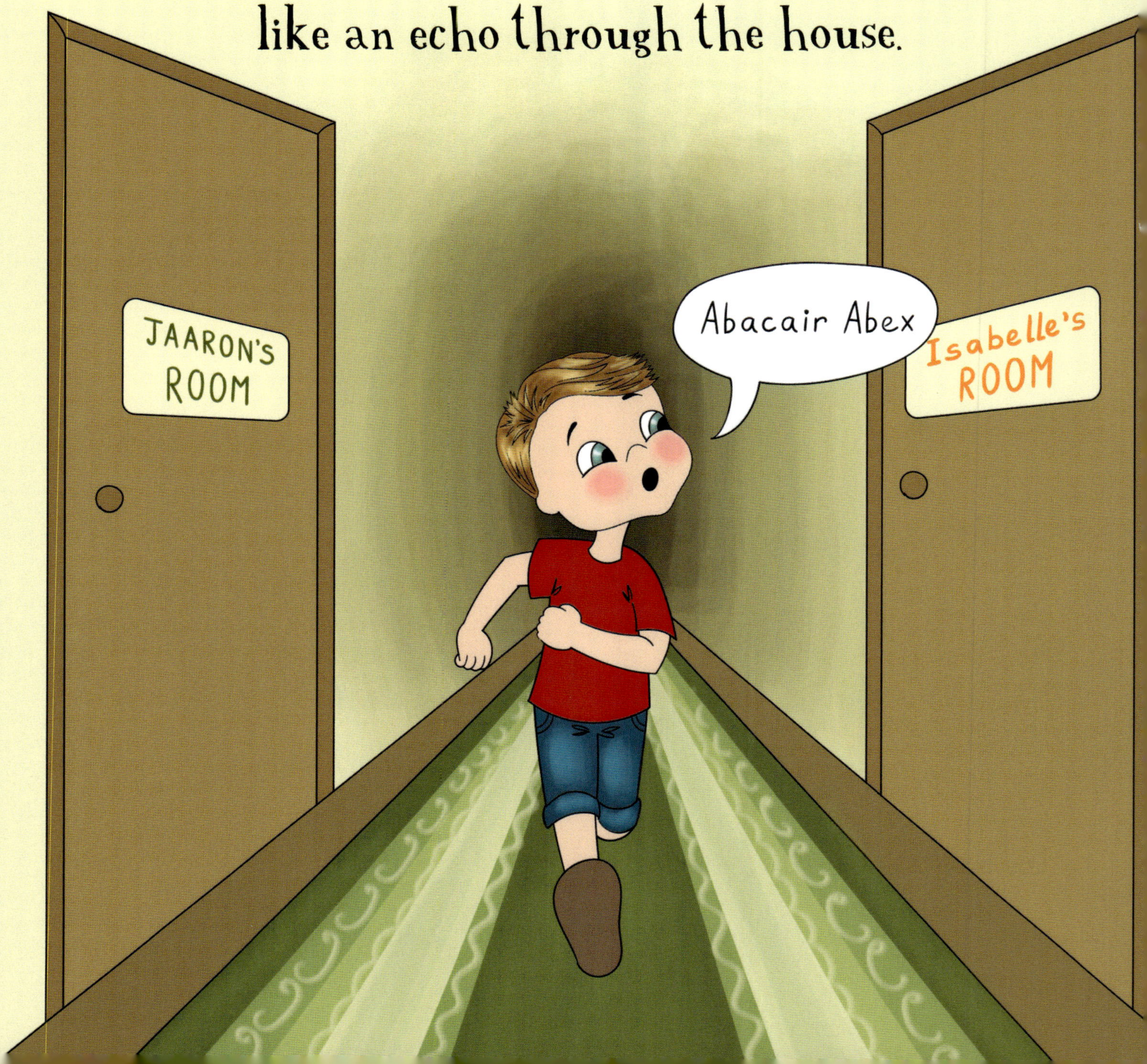

Sometimes it's very loud in there, and other times it's quiet as a mouse.

He is also Ambidextrous (am bi DEX trous),
which may be part of autism, too.
It's when you don't favor one hand or the other.

He knows a lot of sign language.
I had to learn it, too.

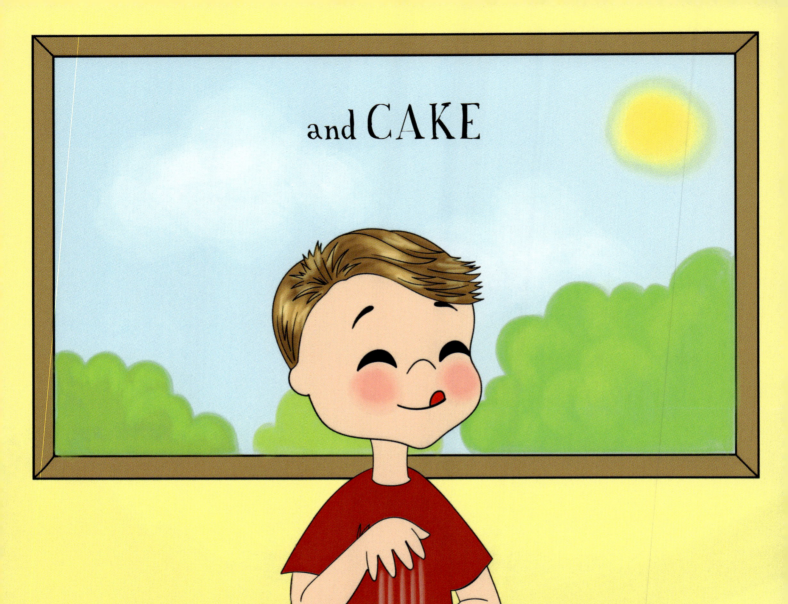

and CAKE

and of course,
I LOVE YOU!

They say because of Autism, he doesn't show affection. But he gives me big hugs and kisses, and to me that is PERFECTION!

The End